MAGGIE AND THE FEROCIOUS BEAST

THE BIG SCARE

Betty Paraskevas

Michael Paraskevas

Simon & Schuster Books for Young Readers

THE Ferocious Beast sat beside the River of Dreams and sniffled a tear that rolled down his cheek and tickled his nose.

"Beast," asked Maggie, "why are you sad?"
"I have a terrible secret," he sighed.
"Tell us," pleaded Hamilton Hocks, "perhaps we can help. That's what friends are for."

"Really?" replied the Beast.

"Hamilton's right," said Maggie.

"Well ... I ... I ... am the ... the Ferocious Beast ... and ... and ..."

"Beast, could you please speed it up a bit," Hamilton complained.

"Take all the time you need," said Maggie.

"Thank you, Maggie." The Beast glared at Hamilton. "As I was saying, I am the Ferocious Beast and . . . and . . ."

"Go on, dear," urged Maggie.

"Sometimes I get scared."

"Gracious sakes, everybody gets scared sometimes. I'm afraid of sea monsters," Hamilton boasted. "WOW!" gasped the Beast. "Have you ever seen one?"

"No," Hamilton admitted.

"I'm afraid of ghosts," Maggie announced.

"Really?" The Beast's eyes grew very large.

"Have you ever seen one?"

"No." Maggie grinned.

"I'm afraid of monsters under my bed," Hamilton whispered.

"Really?" said the Beast. "Have you ever seen one?"

"No." Hamilton looked embarrassed.
"I'm afraid of spaceships from other
galaxies," continued Maggie.
"Really? Have you ever seen one?"

"No," she replied.

"Well, I'm afraid of closet goblins," Hamilton declared.

"Have you ever seen one?" The Beast was sounding a bit bored.

"No," Hamilton confessed.

"Now, tell us what scares you," said Maggie.

The Ferocious Beast shook his head. "No, I just can't. I know you'll laugh at me."

"We won't, we won't," cried Hamilton.

"Promise? Cross your hearts?"
They both agreed.
"Well, I am the Ferocious Beast."
Hamilton groaned. "Yes, we know, we know."
The Beast took a deep breath and spoke one word.

"Mice."

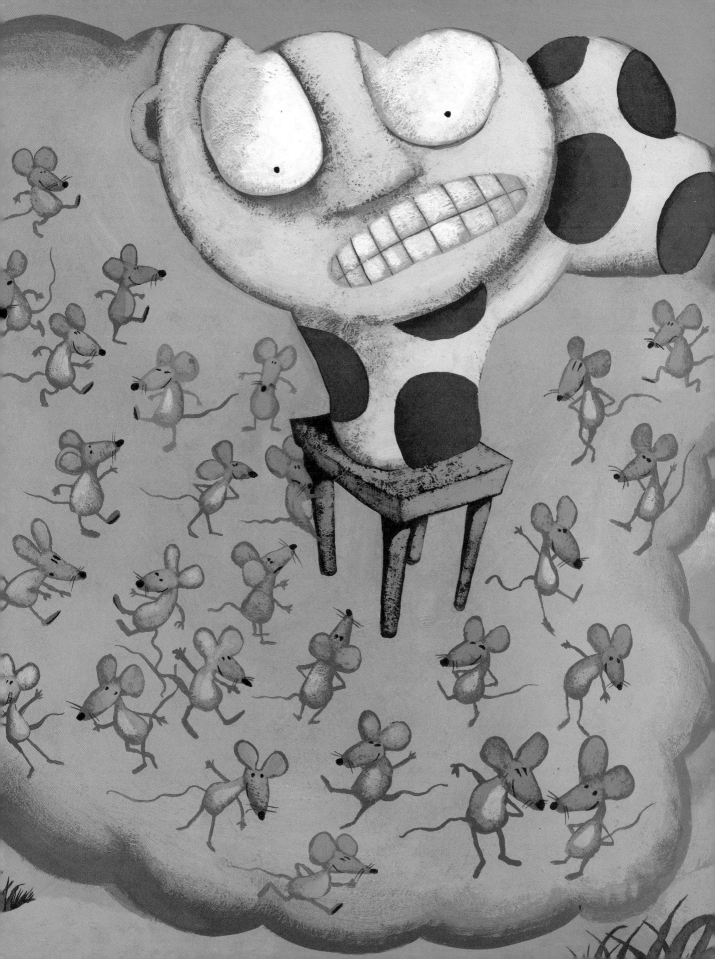

"I'm afraid of mice," he explained.

Maggie and Hamilton began to laugh and the Beast's face turned as red as his polka dots.

"You promised," he wailed.

"Imagine," shouted Hamilton, laughing his special snorting laugh, "the big Ferocious Beast—afraid of a poor itty bitty mousie."

"I guess it is pretty funny for me to be afraid of a little mouse, but . . .

. . . AT LEAST I'VE SEEN ONE!"

"And there's one next to you RIGHT NOW," he cried.

Both Hamilton and Maggie began jumping around, waving their arms, screaming, "A mouse? A mouse? Where? Where? Get away! Get away!"

As the little mouse scampered off, they all began to laugh and Maggie said, "Dear Beast, don't you see? We did make you feel better and that's what good friends are for."

SIMON & SCHUSTER BOOKS FOR YOUNG READERS

An imprint of Simon & Schuster Children's Publishing Division

1230 Avenue of the Americas, New York, New York 10020

Text copyright © 1999 by Rita E. Paraskevas

Illustrations copyright © 1999 by Michael P. Paraskevas

All rights reserved including the right of reproduction
in whole or in part in any form.

SIMON & SCHUSTER BOOKS FOR YOUNG READERS
is a trademark of Simon & Schuster.

The text for this book is set in 18-point Myriad Bold.

The illustrations are rendered in acrylic on paper.

Reprinted by arrangement with Simon & Schuster Books for Young Readers,
an imprint of Simon & Schuster Children's Publishing Division.
Printed in the U.S.A.

10 9 8 7 6 5 4 3 2 1

Library of Congress Cataloging-in-Publication Data

Paraskevas, Betty.
Maggie and the Ferocious Beast : the Big Scare / by Betty
Paraskevas ; illustrated by Michael Paraskevas. — 1st ed.
     p.   cm.
Summary: Maggie and Hamilton help their friend, the
Ferocious Beast, when he confesses that he is afraid of mice.
ISBN 0-689-82489-0
[1. Fear—Fiction. 2. Monsters—Fiction. 3. Mice—Fiction.]
I. Paraskevas, Michael, 1961- , ill. II. Title.
PZ7.P2135Mag 1999
[E]—dc21
98-35946
CIP
AC